Editing by Valerie Sweeten

ISBN-13: 978-1974025176

ISBN-10: 1974025179

Nefertiti & The Great Lake

By

T.L. Johnson

To Tatyana & Taylor

Love Always

Long ago, there lived a young girl who was the most beautiful the world had ever seen. Her name was Princess Nefertiti. There had never been a lovelier princess than her in the entire world. She traveled across the continents so people could admire her stunning beauty, but she had never seen her own face.

Each place she would visit, the people would find an amazing quality of hers to admire.
In Asia, they admired her bronzed skin. "Your skin has been kissed by the sun itself!"

"Thank you," Nefertiti said.

In Italy, they were amazed by her full lips. "Your lips are like honeydew, rich and so full of life!"

"Thank you," Nefertiti said.

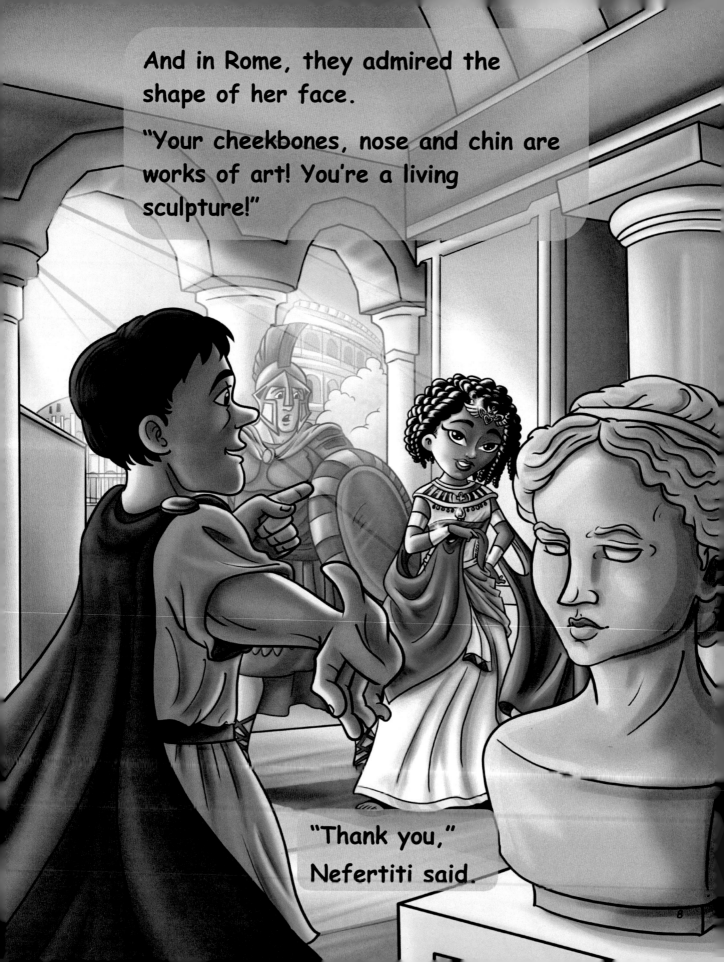

Nefertiti never tired of hearing these compliments, but she still had never seen herself to know if they were true. After her final visit, Nefertiti was ready to go back home to be with her own people. On the way, she stopped by the Great Lake to fill her cup with water.

As she stood on the
shore, the land
locked her legs.

She tried to move, but was unable to. The Great Lake held her prisoner.

"Why have you done this to me?" she asked the Great Lake.

"I have seen many people come and take my water, but you are the most beautiful person I have ever seen, and so I cannot let you go." the lake said.

Nefertiti sighed at this.

"People have told me I am beautiful but I've never seen myself," she said.

"Then you must look into me to see your reflection," the Great Lake demanded.

Nefertiti looked at her reflection in the water. Her cocoa skin danced against the waves. Her eyes were like diamonds in the twilight; her smile as bright as sunbeams.

"I am beautiful!" Nefertiti said.

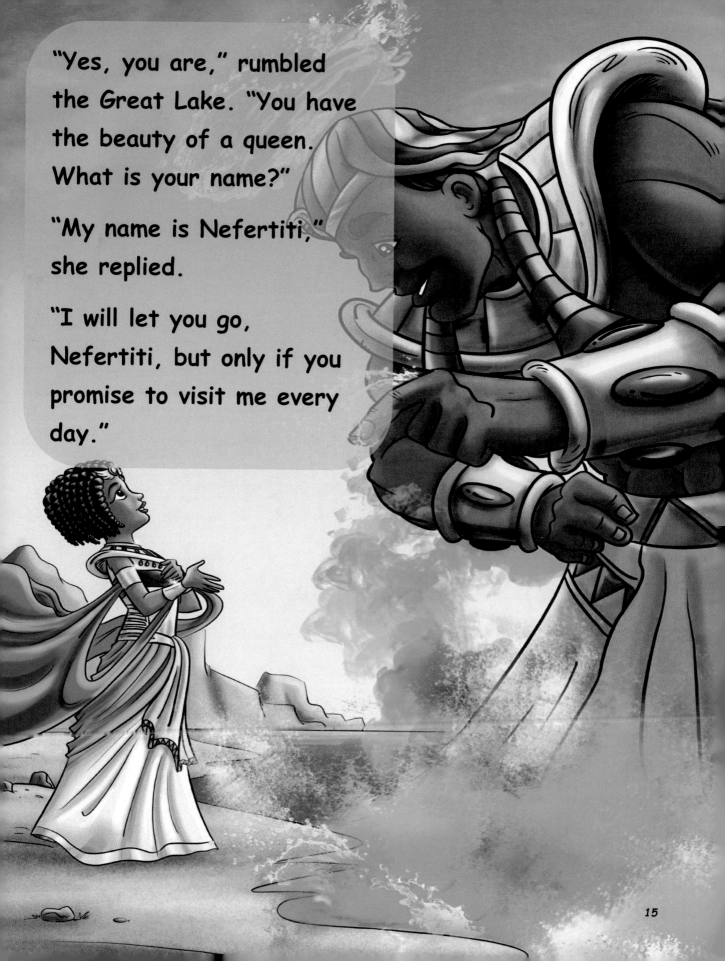

"Yes, you are," rumbled the Great Lake. "You have the beauty of a queen. What is your name?"

"My name is Nefertiti," she replied.

"I will let you go, Nefertiti, but only if you promise to visit me every day."

Nefertiti promised. Each day at noon, she visited the Great Lake. The lake looked at her as she looked at her own reflection.

"Nefertiti, you are by far the most beautiful creature to ever live," the Great Lake said. "But true beauty comes from inside. Your eyes and your heart show you are kind and compassionate. That is why you are the most beautiful girl to ever live."

"Thank you," Nefertiti said. She waved goodbye to the lake and went home.

"It is too cold. You cannot go outside, Nefertiti."

The next day was the first day of winter. There was a terrible storm and no one went outside—except Nefertiti. As she was about to leave, her father, the King, stopped her.

"But Father, I have a promise to keep!" Nefertiti exclaimed.

"I'm sorry, but my answer is no."

Despite her father's warning, Nefertiti still tried to see the Great Lake. She was determined to keep her promise.

But the snow was too deep and the wind too strong. Nefertiti had to return home.

It was the first time in a year that she had not seen the Great Lake.

The next day, the snow melted.

Nefertiti rushed out of her home to see the Great Lake.

When she got there, she was shocked to find the lake frozen.

"Why are you frozen?" Nefertiti asked.

The lake responded, "Because you did not come to see me."

"I am sorry," Nefertiti said, "but I cannot stay here forever. You must melt. The people of my land need your water!"

But the lake was too sad to melt.

23

The King of the land came down to the lake and was shocked as well.

"The people will not live 3 days without the Great Lake. We will all perish. Something must be done. Call the Great Sage."

When the Great Sage appeared, he saw the frozen block of ice and Nefertiti sitting beside the lake. He asked the lake. "Why are you frozen?"

The lake replied, "Because I love Nefertiti and I want to see her forever."

The Great Sage replied, "But she cannot stay here forever, and our land needs the Great Lake! We need water."

Still the lake was still too sad to unfreeze.

Just then, the Great Sage had an idea. He turned to Nefertiti and spoke.

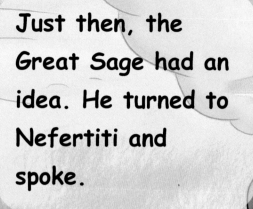

"The Ancient Kings are the only ones with the power to grant your wish. They live in the sky atop our pyramids.

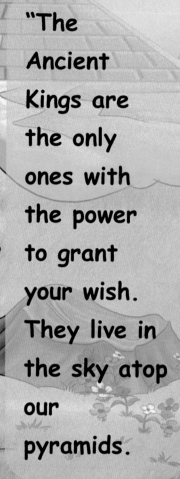

Go to them with your request. You can cut a piece of the lake's ice and climb to the top of the highest pyramid. Then leap into the air and ask the Ancient Kings if you can be together forever."

The Great Lake agreed.

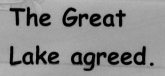

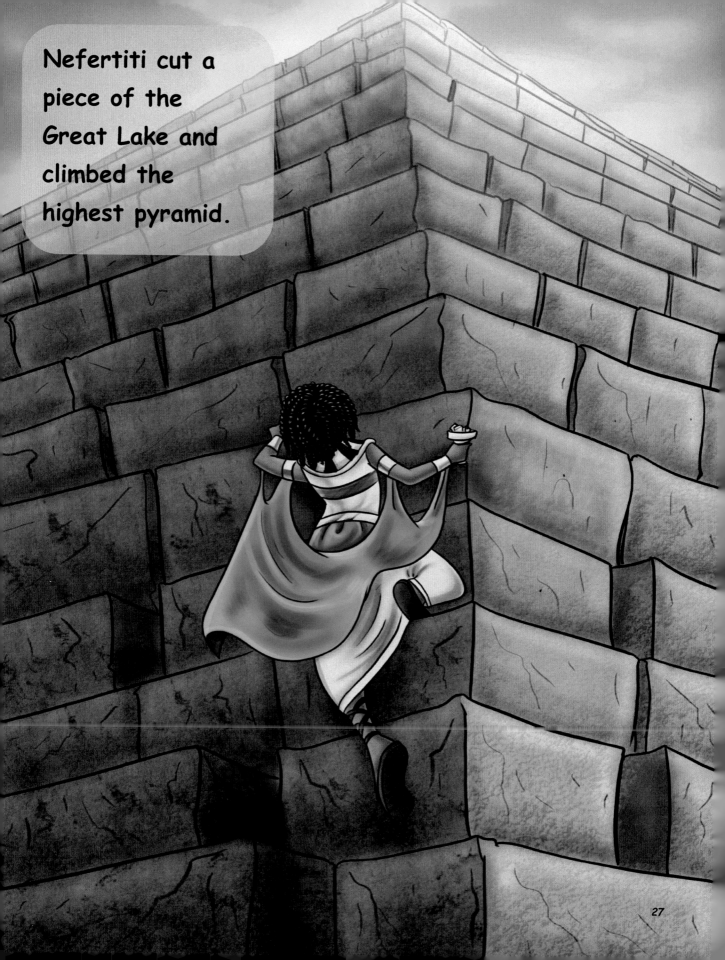

Nefertiti cut a piece of the Great Lake and climbed the highest pyramid.

When she leapt into the air, the Ancient Kings caught her.

"Why are you here, Nefertiti?" the Ancient Kings demanded.

"I love the Great Lake, and the Great Lake loves me, but he will not change into water unless I can be with him forever," said Nefertiti.

The Ancient Kings answered, "The only way you can be with him is if we share your beauty across the land for all the people to have."

Nefertiti agreed readily.

29

Ra, leader of the Ancient Kings then said,

"We made you the most beautiful woman in the world. Why do you want to share our gift with all the children of the world?"

"Everyone tells me I am beautiful on the outside, but the Great Lake showed me that my true beauty is inside," said Nefertiti, "and I want the people to be just like me, beautiful inside and out."

The Ancient Kings were pleased with her answer. They took the block of ice and turned it into a cloud.

The cloud took all of Nefertiti's beauty and traveled across the land. It rained her beauty down on all the little children of the world until they became as beautiful as Nefertiti, both inside and out.

The Ancient Kings took another part of the Great Lake and transformed it into a mirror. Now Nefertiti and the Great Lake could always see each other.

The lake was so happy that it melted and the people came to use its water again.

"Thank you!" the people called out to Nefertiti.

Nefertiti smiled to see her beauty in all the children of the world. And from this day forward, anytime you look into the reflection of the Great Lake or any mirror anywhere, you are looking into the beauty of Nefertiti and the beauty within every child in the world.

-The End

34

Made in the USA
Columbia, SC
17 December 2022

74188999R00020